A Mysterious
Evening in Vienna

By John R. Teevan III

Table of Contents

JOHN R. TEEVAN III

Atomic Secrets

The Soviet rocket scientist met with the covert agent in the café in Berlin. West Berlin? East Berlin? We don't know. That information was classified.

Agent Harderman had bought off one of the rocket scientists working behind the Iron Curtain. Dr. Ivanov had access to the plans for the atomic facility that, among other things, would build nuclear missiles that Moscow would aim directly at Washington, DC. With access to these secret plans, Dr. Ivanov was willing to exchange them for an astronomical sum. The amount Harderman gave Dr. Ivanov was enough dollars to build the entire atomic facility itself. But now without the plans ... or the planner: the coffee was poisoned.

Dr. Ivanov dropped his coffee cup and watched it shatter on the floor. With exasperated eyes, he glanced with fear at the agent. "You?- You?-"

"Sorry," Harderman said, as Dr. Ivanov collapsed to the floor. "I had to cover my traces. But keep the money. There's plenty of that where that came from." And the agent took the briefcase with Soviet atomic secrets and walked away.

Taking the train back West, Agent James Harderman kept an extra eye out for followers. For followers from any country. From anywhere. For *everyone*.

In fact, a little bit too *much* of an eye out.

He suddenly gazed upon the most beautiful lady he had ever seen. From head to toe, she was entrancing. All language – and mind you, as a covert operatives agent, he knew quite a few languages – all language was lost from his entranced mind. He dropped his briefcase, which quietly thudded on the floor of the coach heading through Prague. At lightning speed. Things can get overlooked when passing at lightning speed. Including the fact that he had just dropped the briefcase containing papers with atomic secrets that could destroy the world should they fall into the wrong hands. Or, better yet, fall to the floor.

But Agent Harderman was so taken aback by his natural attraction to this woman that he momentarily lost all sense of time, place, perspective and identity. He was not Covert Agent James Harderman of the U.S. CIA. He was a lover and she was his soulmate. And-

Bam! Suddenly the burst of a machine gun struck James, and he fell backwards. Away from her. Away from his future. Away from his love. Away from his briefcase. Away from the papers containing the atomic secrets that could destroy the world.

And he blacked out.

Beep! Beep! Beep! The heart rate monitor was the first thing James heard. He must be in a hospital. Somewhere in Switzerland. And-

Her!! It was the lady on the train! "Where?- Wh-?"

"Sh!" She told him. "They will find you if you make noise! And -"

"Where am I?"

"We're hiding you in my home in Spain. Soviet agents seized the train in Czechoslovakia and shot you."

"And who are you?"

"Maria."

"Are you a spy? A civilian? A Soviet? A NATO operative? A -"

"I am Maria. A Spaniard. Nothing more."

"Can I trust you?" he probed.

"How should I know? Why should I care? How should I know who you choose to trust or not?"

"My briefcase!" Harderman exclaimed as he suddenly realized he was missing the papers that could unleash the plans for an atomic facility.

"Don't worry."

"But-"

"They're in good hands," she reassured.

"Do you have them?"

"They're in good hands."

"But-" he stammered.

"No time for details. We must move on now. Hurry!" And they got into a car and headed for Paris.

Border police. James had bloody bandages wrapped around

his left arm where he had been shot. What will they do?

"Are you together?" asked the border agent.

"Yes," responded Maria.

And they lived the rest of their days together in France.

So how does the story end? Anyone who saves the world from nuclear armageddon deserves a happily ever after. James and Maria got married in Paris. They had an elaborate wedding at the beautiful Notre-Dame Cathedral. To protect their identities they were married under the names on their counterfeit French passports. After a career of killing spies and high-stakes secret nuclear negotiations, James retired to a peaceful life of playing boules in the Jardin du Luxembourg in Paris. Maria wrote adventure novels about falling in love with mysterious spies on trains and the exciting adventures that result from these encounters. She wrote under a pseudonym in her native Spanish so none of her new friends in Paris would know about her past. Maria and James had a long and happy marriage. There was a sense of freedom they won by giving up their previous identities – their past – and living the dream they chose for themselves. They loved each other more and more each day and were forever grateful they met on the train in Prague.

What about the atomic secrets? The briefcase that disappeared on the train? What happened to the papers that could destroy the world?

During the mêlée that ensued during the shooting on the train, the papers were victim of a defenestration. They flew out the window during the chaos. Another Defenestration of Prague[1]. The Soviet Czech civil authorities had over-chlorinated the drinking water. So when the papers reached the gutter, they disappeared in the chlorine-heavy water. Without the plans the atomic facility was never built. Everyone lived happily ever after. Including James and Maria.

---

[1] The word "defenestration" means to throw someone or something out the window. It is a really cool word to write and say, mostly because it is so uber specific in its meaning. In 1618, the Second Defenestration of Prague – where three men were literally thrown out the window – started the Thirty Years' War. While the train carrying James and Maria was passing through Prague, the papers flew out the window. What better occasion to use the word "defenestration"? This could be the Third Defenestration of Prague.

The Eternal Emperor

The emperor turned to his most trusted – but not trustworthy – advisor.

"Are you sure, Marcus?"

"Our spies estimate its reliability to be at 70%, Mister Emperor."

The wise, but not shrewd, emperor scratched his head, muttering over and over again "70%. 70%. 70%." Finally he interrupted his thoughts: "But a C- is failing."

"70% is majority. Majority rules," responded the advisor.

"So if we know we have a majority, let's present it to the Senate and they will approve it. And 70% is filibuster-proof."

"Mister Emperor!! A public debate?? About a topic like this?? The public does not need to know. This is not a public matter, or *res publica*. Leave the *res publica*[2] to the Republic. But this

---

[2] The word "republic" comes from Latin *res + publica* literally meaning "public matter/thing." See Douglas Harper, *Online Etymology Dictionary*, s.v. "republic," Accessed August 8, 2017, http://www.etymonline.com/index.php ?term=republic&allowed_in_frame=0. The play on words about leaving the "public matters" to the Republic is more than just a nerd joke for those of us who like etymology and historical linguistics. It is a debate about the very nature of a republic – literally "the public thing." How open should government be when discrete, efficient and decisive action is required? How much of public administration should be public? This dilemma is articulated in the dialogue between the emperor and his adviser Marcus.

matter requires your discrete and decisive action."

The emperor scratched his head again in deep contemplation. "How did you find this potion again?"

"Like I said, Mister Emperor, there's a 70% chance that the immortality potion is in Alexandria."

"But how do you know?"

"Remember that guy who's been cleaning toilets for a living for my younger brother's factory?"

"Yes."

"And remember that he cleaned toilets for my father when my father ran the factory?"

"Yes …"

"And remember when my grandfather passed away, at that time, this guy was cleaning toilets at my grandfather's factory too?"

"Mm-hmm."

"Well it turns out, he's been an employee of that factory for seven generations."

"What did he do before he was cleaning toilets at that factory?"

"I don't know. That was before the industrial revolution, and my family's factory didn't exist then. I don't know where he worked then. All I know is that he was alive then. Before the factory was built, seven generations ago."

The wise, but not shrewd, emperor scratched his head, again in deep contemplation.

"If this guy holds the secret to immortality, then why in the world is he still scrubbing toilets for a living?" the emperor asked. "He could be ruling the world!"

"That's exactly why. He likes to keep a low profile."

"What do you mean?"

"The story goes, in Antiquity, this guy was alive. The Egyptians learned about his immortality potion and came after him. After all, Pharaoh is god and you can't be more powerful, or have a better afterlife, than Pharaoh. Pharaoh sought to obtain this potion."

"Did he?"

"They caught the man. But he had hidden the potion in one of the millions of blocks of the pyramids."

"So what happened?"

"Pharaoh ordered the man tortured until he told where the potion was. Realizing that he would spend thousands and thousands of years in pain and never die, the man escaped, vowing to spend the rest of his life in hiding. In a place where no one would ever remember him or notice his indefinite presence."

"So he decided to scrub toilets for a living of all things?" asked the emperor.

"Well, he wanted to not be noticed. He's been in my family for seven generations and nobody even noticed that was unusual. So yes, he succeeded in getting what he wanted."

"So what do we do about this potion?" asked the emperor.

Marcus presented a 57-page directive. "Mister Emperor, you can read all 57 pages of this plan and take 3 years to execute it. Or you can just sign this executive order," Marcus presented a slip of parchment to the Emperor with a quill, "and I'll take care of it all for you."

The emperor sighed and scratched his head, deep in thought.

"Is the potion a blessing? A curse? A threat? An asset?" he mused.

Marcus responded, "Well, we can't govern him, because the State cannot control his life and death.[3] And we can't execute him for treason because he can't die."

"Mmmmmmmmm ... how about this: I'm retiring next summer from my position as emperor. Why don't you just have him take my job?"

Marcus' jaw dropped. "Mister Emperor, you want the

---

[3] French philosopher Jacques Derrida and French historian Élisabeth Roudinesco analyzed the role of the State over the life and death of its subjects. In a way, the sovereignty of a ruler depends on his control over the life and death of his subjects - his power to execute or pardon. A matter of life and death. Fear is a threat to one's very existence. It is this very Machiavellian fear – fear of death, fear of execution – that keeps his subjects in line. It is the very base of any monarch's power. For example, the French Revolution was legitimized when the new regime guillotined the king. In a sense, the Revolutionary regime had control over Louis XVI's life or death, just as, in the Ancien Régime, he had power over the life or death of his subjects. Anyone who dared challenge the authority of the king – i.e. attempt assassination – was drawn and quartered in a spectacularly painful showing of the king's power over the life and death of his subjects. See Jacques Derrida & Élisabeth Roudinesco, *For What Tomorrow ... A Dialogue*, Jeff Fort (Translator), (Stanford, CA: Stanford University Press, 2004), 144.

empire to be governed by a toilet-scrubber?!'"

The emperor, wise but not shrewd, slowly replied, "Mmmmmm ... yeah."

Suddenly, Marcus, trusted but not trustworthy, pulled out a dagger and mortally stabbed the emperor. The emperor died. Marcus was shrewd but not wise. The toilet-cleaning man arrived, mixed bleach and ammonia and let the fumes spread throughout the emperor's office. Marcus suffocated, leaving the toilet-scrubbing man still alive, coughing for breath but able to escape the toxic chemicals without dying. He opened a window for fresh air and climbed onto the balcony. Only then did he realize that, as he stood on the balcony, thousands of citizens had gathered to see the commotion. Upon his arrival in their view, they cheered on the new emperor. And all humanity lived in peace for the rest of his eternal reign.

Melancholy Euphoria

Today was the day the two lovers would part. Sam and Luisa planned to meet at the dock where she would board the ship back to São Paulo. Sam was going to miss her with all his heart. They may never be in the same country again. It was 1917 and the world was at war. Nothing was certain except one thing: she was as beautiful as the first night he met her. Luisa's long black hair gently cascaded down her shoulders. She was thin, yet she had curves in every place that would melt any man's heart. Talk about heart, she had the heart – the very soul – of life. The spirit of Brazilian Carnival. The unending joy that never ceases. The dance that keeps dancing. The emotion that melts the minds of men.

Luisa, with suitcase in hand, approached her lover. "Samuel," she said with a seductive Portuguese accent, "I don't think I will ever forget you no matter how far I go."

"Will you come back to visit?" he asked.

There was a pause. In lieu of words, Luisa approached Sam and planted a luscious kiss on his lips. They embraced, and for a moment their two souls were one.

The steam ship's whistle blew, indicating it was time to board.

"Samuel, I love you," she said.

And with that she vanished into the shadows.

What did Sam feel? What did he do? He was madly in love with Luisa. He did not *do*, he just felt. He stood there, a million thoughts going through his head. Despair, hope, love, grief, melancholy euphoria. The lover who was loved and will have a memory for the rest of his life.

Some moments in life are better as starry-eyed memories. The emotion – the joy – of love is forever preserved, like a fossil in amber. There is no wedding-planning drama, no divorce fights, no in-laws, no terrible two's. Just a memory that will be forever shining bright in his heart.

That is what Sam thought. That is what Sam felt. But what did he do?

Sam went for a walk alone on the pier. The steam from the steam ships created a dreamy ambiance, the claire-obscure nature of Sam's emotions.

What did he miss most? The kiss? Her heart of gold? Her curves? Her radiant personality? If he could buy jewelry for her – all the diamonds in the world – her personality would shine no more than it already shines. She radiates life itself.

What does one do? The two lovers will probably never see each other again. Post cards can fulfill the proverbial "Don't forget to write." But what about more? What about the euphoria and joy of love? The feeling of caring compassion? What can fulfill that need for being together?

The steam ship, with Luisa on board, headed towards the horizon – beyond the reaches of the human senses. She would soon be out of sight. The horizon is the limit that separates our visible world from our imagination.

She may have been thousands and thousands of miles away from him, but Luisa would always be near to Sam's heart.

JOHN R. TEEVAN III

A Note on Melancholy Euphoria

Will their destinies allow them to cross paths again? Will Sam and Luisa ever be in the same place at the same time ever again? Will the War to End All Wars ever be finished? What good is it to live in this world if we don't know if we will be killed tomorrow? Tomorrow – in all its mysteriousness. Sometimes anticipation is more romantic than the actual meeting itself.

1917 was chosen very intentionally for the setting of "Melancholy Euphoria." 1917 ... mysterious in its ambiguity. This was the year that the United States entered World War One. Did Sam know he was going to be drafted? Will he go off to war and die in the trenches, never to see Luisa again? Or was this earlier in the year, before Congress declared war on Germany: before Sam had any idea of what lied in store?

Likewise, Luisa is no less immune to fate. Unrestricted submarine warfare was sinking even civilian ships. Will Luisa's ship be sunk by a German U-boat? Will she reach São Paulo? Will she make it home to read the love letter that Sam will mail to her? If Sam never hears from her again because her ship sank: he will die too - in his heart.

Just as this story, ink on paper, the fruit of the human imagination, is mysterious in its uncertainty, so too is life mysterious in destiny and fate. We do not know what will happen tomorrow. Rather than fear uncertainty, let us relish the moments, embrace the future and never stop dreaming.

17

JOHN R. TEEVAN III

Diplomacy à la Vodka

Translated into English Throughout

"Your excellency, are you –"

"Nope, I'm just drunk."

"But – "

"I'm putting you in charge of the negotiations. Don't start World War Three." And he passed out.

The Under Minister of Foreign Affairs stared at his boss, Soviet Foreign Minister Molotov, who was now collapsed on the couch. "Well, I guess it's up to me to handle the negotiations," he mused.

The Prussian diplomats arrived in Geneva. And the Russians arrived … three weeks late because they needed to take the train from Leningrad through Central Europe.

"You're late," said the Germans, who had driven from Berlin and arrived early, 3 days ahead of the scheduled meeting time just in case they got a flat tire. Germans are always on time. Germans are always early.

There are times when the dictatorship of the proletariat is worse than the dictatorship of tyrants. At least the kaiser runs his government on time. Meanwhile Lenin is drunk on vodka.

The negotiations began. And continued. And went nowhere. Because there was no translator. The Germans made propositions in Deutsch and the Russians confusedly responded in Russkiy. And the press kept saying, "It's Greek to Me!"

"What the hell is going on in Europe?" demanded Churchill. "Why can't the European Union get their shit together?"

"The affairs of Europe are the affairs of Europe. *You* are an *island*," said de Gaulle. Although it sounded more like [zee affairez œv œrʌp aʁ zee affairez œv œrʌp. juw aʁ ʌn ajlənd].

"I know. Thank god for Brexit," said Churchill.

Vladimir Lenin sent a cable to his Foreign Minister. "How are the negotiations with the Germans going? Stop. Report back when your hangover is done. Stop. Awaiting news from the Eastern Front. Stop."

Molotov muttered, "Damn. The proletariat has awoken. Which means I need to get up." The Russian foreign minister pulled himself up off of the couch, made his way through the maze of vodka bottles and proceeded to put on his bow tie and 3 piece suit and top hat. As he sobered up on his way to the League of Nations downtown, he asked the cab driver, "What year is it?" The taxi driver replied, "This is an asynchronous piece of fiction, you idiot. There *is* no year!"

As the Soviet foreign minister arrived he asked his Under Minister, "Did you start World War Three?" "No, your excellency." "Ok, then you did a good job." "Spasibo." "Pozhaluysta."

A Note on Diplomacy à la Vodka

This whole story takes place in the mindset of a dreamy, intoxicated fantasy in Interwar Europe. I began writing the original in French, then switched to English, then back to French for specific passages that are best expressed in a dreamy foreign language.

The stream-of-consciousness story about diplomacy lost in translation seems very fitting for a work that alternates between languages it is written in. I am including the following original version written in French and English because that best expresses the thoughts and emotions that I wish to express. I do want all interested readers to be able to access my writing, and the immediately preceding pages are the version I translated into English throughout.

I wrote this following Brexit and the disunion of the European Union.

The title "Diplomacy à la Vodka" expresses this mixture of drunk confusion of foreign languages with international negotiations - as though diplomacy were a dish that could be served like penne à la vodka.

Diplomacy à la vodka

Original Written in Mix of French & English

« Monsieur le ministre, êtes-vous – »

« Ben non, j'suis simplement saoul »

« Mais – »

« Je vous mets en charge des négociations. Commence pas la troisième guerre mondiale ». Et il s'est évanoui.

The Under Minister of Foreign Affairs stared at his boss, Soviet Foreign Minister Molotov, who was now collapsed on the couch. "Well, I guess it's up to me to handle the negotiations," he mused.

Les diplomates prussiens arrivaient à Genève. Et les Russes arrivaient … trois semaines en retard parce qu'ils devaient prendre le train de Leningrad à travers l'Europe centrale.

"You're late," said the Germans, who had driven from Berlin and arrived early, 3 days ahead of the scheduled meeting time just in case they got a flat tire. Germans are always on time. Germans are always early.

Il y a des moments que la dictature du prolétariat est pire que la dictature des tyrans. At least the kaiser runs his government on time. Meanwhile Lenin is drunk on vodka.

Alors les négociations commencent. Et continuent. Et vont nulle part. Because there is no translator. The Germans make propositions in Deutsch and the Russians confusedly respond in Russkiy. And the press keeps saying, "It's Greek to Me!"

"What the hell is going on in Europe?" demanded Churchill. "Why can't the European Union get their shit together?"

"The affairs of Europe are the affairs of Europe. *You* are an *island*," said de Gaulle. Although it sounded more like [zee affairez œv œrʌp aʁ zee affairez œv œrʌp. juw aʁ ʌn ajlənd].

"I know. Thank god for Brexit," said Churchill.

Vladimir Lenin sent a cable to his Foreign Minister. "How are the negotiations with the Germans going? Stop. Report back when your hangover is done. Stop. Awaiting news from the Eastern Front. Stop."

Molotov muttered, "Damn. The proletariat has awoken. Which means I need to get up." The Russian foreign minister pulled himself up off of the couch, made his way through the maze of vodka bottles and proceeded to put on his bow tie and 3 piece suit and top hat. As he sobered up on his way to the League of Nations downtown, he asked the cab driver, "What year is it?" The taxi driver replied, "This is an asynchronous piece of fiction, you idiot. There *is* no year!"

As the Soviet foreign minister arrived he asked his Under Minister, "Did you start World War Three?" "No, your excellency." "Ok, then you did a good job." "Spasibo." "Pozhaluysta."

The Spy's White Dress

Thousands of soldiers rallied their support to General Santiago, the new dictator of the republic of Florina in Latin America.

The opposition party fled the capital, before being massacred by the national guard. They escaped to the jungle. The head of the opposition party, Alejandro, and his lover, Clara, swore to never abandon their passion for their cause – nor their passion for one another.

All of a sudden, a spy, Cecilia, emerged from the shadows of the jungle. She wore a beautiful white dress that covered her body but not her bare feet nor her thin, delicate shoulders. Her white dress did not hide the dark and bloody mission she had carried out. White, the noble color of innocence, was far from the treasonous plot committed by the spy wearing that white dress. Cecilia had infiltrated enemy lines – won the trust of General Santiago – only to return to the opposition party. Why was she wearing a white dress? Was it her wedding night? Or her vengeful honeymoon? Regardless of her connection to General Santiago, her true loyalty was married to the opposition party.

Cecilia approached Alejandro. "The die is cast," she whispered. Alejandro reacted with a smile of sinister pleasure. "When do we invade?" he asked. She responded, "Now."

Suddenly, a siren rang out. It was an emergency siren, followed by the shouts of an enraged crowd, shocked upon learning of the death of General Santiago.

Cecilia was just as much a spy as she was an assassin.

General Santiago's death was the moment the opposition part had been waiting for to take back the capital and depose the military junta when it was at its weakest point – during the power vacuum following General Santiago's death. "Our time has come!" proclaimed Alejandro, "To arms!!" And he raised his gun over his head. His supporters shouted, "Long live the republic! Long live Alejandro! Long live Florina!"

The forces of order fought against the forces of opposition. In the streets. In the mud. In the fields. In the blood.

At last, the fighting was over. The flag was raised – proudly – high above the Capitol. Peace and order were restored. And Alejandro and Clara rested together beneath a palm tree in peace and in paradise.

A Note on The Spy's White Dress

How does "The Spy's White Dress" end? What exactly happens? I have intentionally left the ending ambiguous. Which flag was raised? Did Alejandro win and he is relaxing in paradise to celebrate his victory? Did he perish, and he rests in peace in heaven? In the original French, the word "paradis" can mean either "heaven" or "paradise." It is not for me to decide how you should interpret the ending. Rely on your own creative imagination to choose for yourself. The mysteriousness of the ending allows you to imagine incredible endings that could not be contained in black and white words on paper – only in the human imagination.

When writing, some ideas come to me more naturally and are expressed more fluently in French. "The Spy's White Dress" was originally written in French as « La Robe blanche de l'espionne ». As with any translation, the original is always more fresh, creative, expressive, complete, and effective at moving the reader – swaying them with the essence of the passion I am trying to capture. I am providing the English version first because I want this story to be accessible to my readers, but I would be remiss if I did not include the original French version which best communicates the thoughts I am trying to express. The French version is found after this note.

On the following page is a drawing of Florina, to illustrate "The Spy's White Dress." This was hastily drawn on a napkin, as a quick, rough sketch at the café during writing group. Yet it is the best illustration of the thoughts and passions I am trying to express because it was created during the moment of inspiration. In the bottom-left corner is the beautiful spy, Cecilia, wearing her white dress, with her bloody dagger. On the top-right is the flag being raised. Or is it being lowered? Which flag is it? The bottom-right shows the palm tree referenced at the end.

La Robe blanche de l'espionne

Des milliers de soldats ont engagé leur fidélité au général Santiago, le nouveau dictateur de la république de Florina en Amérique latine.

Le parti d'opposition a fui la capitale, avant d'être massacré par la garde nationale. Ils se sont échappés dans la jungle. Le chef du parti d'opposition, Alejandro, et son amant, Clara, ont juré de ne jamais abandonner leur passion pour leur cause – ni leur passion pour l'un et l'autre.

Tout d'un coup, une espionne, Cécile, est sortie de l'ombre mystérieuse de la jungle. Elle portait une belle robe blanche qui couvrait son corps mais pas ses jambes nues ni ses épaules minces et délicates. Sa robe blanche ne cachait pas les activités noires, sombres et sanglantes qu'elle avait faites. Blanc, la couleur noble de l'innocence, était loin du complot traître que l'espionne habillée dans cette robe blanche vient de faire. Cécile avait infiltré des lignes ennemies – a gagné la confiance du général Santiago – seulement pour revenir au parti d'opposition. Pourquoi portait-elle une robe blanche ? Était-ce sa nuit de noces ? Ou son voyage de noces de vengeance ? Quoi que soit sa connexion au général Santiago, sa vraie loyauté était mariée avec le parti d'opposition.

Cécile s'est approchée d'Alejandro. « Les jeux sont faits » elle a chuchoté. Il réagissait avec un sourire sinistre de plaisir. « À quelle heure envahissons-nous ? » Alejandro a demandé. Elle a répondu « maintenant ».

Tout d'un coup, une sirène s'est éclatée dans les champs. C'était une sirène d'urgence, qui était suivie par les cris d'une foule folle, insensée par l'apprentissage de la mort du général Santiago.

Cécile était autant espionne qu'assassine.

Le parti d'opposition attendait ce moment – la mort du général Santiago – pour regagner le contrôle de la capitale et déposer la junte quand c'était dans sa position la plus faible – pendant le vide politique de la mort du général Santiago. « L'heure nous est arrivée » a proclamé Alejandro, « Aux armes ! » Et il levait son fusil au-dessus de sa tête. Ses supporters criaient « Vive la république ! Vive Alejandro ! Vive Florina ! »

Les forces d'ordre luttaient contre les forces d'opposition. Dans les champs. Dans les rues. Dans le sang. Dans la boue.

Enfin, la lutte a fini. Le drapeau s'élevait – avec fierté – au-dessus de la capitale. La paix et l'ordre étaient rétablis. Et Alejandro et Clara reposaient ensemble sous un palmier en paix et au paradis.

International Territory

"International Territory" reads the sign at the entrance to the UN Headquarters. What happens if a crime is committed in international territory? Whose jurisdiction is it? By what authority can they pursue justice?

"Well, we can't just turn Sebastian over to the NYPD," mused the Secretariat's chief legal counsel. "Cleary they don't have jurisdiction in this small slice of Manhattan. But this legal loophole – how do we prosecute Sebastian – and by what authority can we put him on trial?"

"There *is* no legal precedent," concluded the Secretary-General, "So we must make one."

The General Assembly was summoned to adopt a resolution and create a policy to pursue justice in this type of jurisdiction. The representatives of Bylvania shouted out in support of Sebastian. The representatives from Vlanistan interjected to criticize the criminal. The Sakian representative gave an impassioned plea to support his ally who was under attack at the podium. As chaos ensued, the interpreters, overwhelmed with so many voices to translate all at once, shut down to silence. International communication ends, embassies close and talking ceases right before a war. And it looked like this spark set off at the UN General Assembly was about to ignite World War Three.

The Secretary-General promptly withdrew his resolution. "Crimes are a threat to security, and as such should be handled by the Security Council." The resolution was presented to the Security Council. Russia boycotted the meeting out of protest, just like the Korean War.[4] China and the U.S. decided that whatever one voted the other would agree – thanks to Walmart they were best friends and international trade connected their economies in ways that made it impossible for them to not work in the same direction. China's economy may be communist in theory but it is the most capitalist nation on earth in practice. And money makes the world go round. France and England, still getting over the Hundred Years' War, held a grudge and agreed that whatever way the Brits would vote the French would vote the opposite, and vice versa. Having one of the permanent members of the UN Security Council vetoing the resolution, it failed. Justice was not established.

"Hmm – how about the International Court of Justice?" mused the Secretary-General.

"But, your honor, that's only for crimes against humanity," responded the chief legal counsel.

"A crime against a human *is* a crime against humanity."

"Original jurisdiction … it's agreed."

Sebastian was taken to The Hague for trial before the International Court of Justice.

---

[4] During the Korean War, Russia protested by boycotting the UN. This ironically backfired. Russia's abstention prevented a veto from any of the 5 permanent members of the Security Council. This allowed the intervention to be a fully-supported police action under the aegis of the United Nations.

The presiding judge began the trial by addressing the Secretary-General. "Your honor, you idiot! You just spent our precious budget on buying airfare to the Netherlands for Sebastian?! He's probably off using marijuana with the prostitutes right now, having the time of his life! You call this a punishment?!"

"We had to extradite him to your court."

"Deport him, is more like it! Sebastian is an Ambassador Plenipotentiary to the United Nations. He has diplomatic immunity. We can't punish him. He's immune from our system of justice. He's a diplomat."

The presiding judge and the Secretary-General looked at each other in the eye and smiled. Their grin indicated that they both knew the plan. A cruel, sinister, pleasurable way of exacting sweet justice.

Sebastian was returned to the General Assembly, and then escorted out of the UN Headquarters – out of international territory. The NYPD approached Sebastian. "May I see your visa, sir?"

"I *have* no visa to enter the U.S. I came to international territory."

"But you ain't there now," said the officer. "And you have no visa to come to the U.S. We have to deport you."

"Great! I'm going back to Florina!"[5]

---

[5] I wanted to pick a made-up country for Sebastian to represent. Florina is the country where "The Spy's White Dress" takes place. See page 25.

"No, sir. You don't have a citizenship passport from Florina. You have a diplomatic passport with a visa to international territory. We'll have to return you to international territory. Currently our State Department does not recognize Movrastan."

"But that's a no man's land!"

"It is the disputed territory between two countries. Because you have disturbed the peace your punishment is keeping the peace. Congratulations, you've just been hired back to the UN. You'll join the UN peacekeeping force in the disputed region."

"Ok, I'll accept this."

And there were never any more crimes ever again. At least not within the UN jurisdiction. All of the other diplomats were afraid of getting shipped off to the landmine-infested no man's land. So everyone behaved. The Secretary-General succeeded in creating a policy – and more importantly in deterring future crime. And the United Nations set the trend, as it should, for all countries of the world – with a crime rate of 0% within UN Headquarters for all eternity.

Today Was the Day

Today was the day. For 37 years the Cedrians had been living in fear – in hiding – preparing for the day that the soldiers would find them. Escape procedures had been planned in detail, years and years in advance. In advance of today. When the army would finish eliminating them.

37 years ago, a new governor-general was nominated to lead the province. Every day that he was in power he encroached further and further on the Cedrians. They were a minority group making up 25% of the population. Then, suddenly, plague struck. Panic ensued. To unite the people and find a common enemy, the governor-general declared all Cedrians to be outlaws. They were the scapegoats. Was the governor-general aware that the Cedrians had nothing to do with causing the plague? Was he cruelly – and unjustly – blaming this powerless minority to find a scapegoat and bolster his support by uniting the people against an enemy – even if it is a made-up enemy?

Or was he just not connected enough to this soft-spoken minority group – so small that you would never even notice them. If every single Cedrian wrote a letter to their representatives at the Provincial Assembly, the letters would be unopened because there were so few of them compared to all the other mail received on a daily basis.

So was the governor-general cruel and destructive? Or was he uninformed – both about his subjects and about the fundamentals of epidemiology?

To be honest, it doesn't matter. He still did what he did. Even if we want to delve into his head and study the decision-making of his psychology, psychology is the study of behavior, not intentions. Whether he was cruelly wanting to hurt the Cedrians or whether he just was such a stupid politician that he sincerely thought the Cedrians had brought on the plague – either way he did the same thing. And what he did was start a genocide.

The Cedrians lost their citizenship. Police were replaced with heavily-armed soldiers from the army trained to gun down men, women and children identified as belonging to the Cedrian ethnicity. More humanity was killed by the purge than ever was by the plague. The Provincial Assembly re-elected the governor-general – partly because he had united the province on this witch hunt, bolstering his power. And partly out of fear. Because anyone who speaks up – any assemblyman who does not whole-heartedly endorse the governor-general's re-election – is a traitor, an enemy, and will probably end up massacred as mercilessly as the Cedrians.

And then it ended. The victims were purged. The massacre accomplished what it wanted to. And for 37 years nobody ever heard about the Cedrians. Except the Cedrians themselves. A group of them had survived and went into hiding, vowing never to be seen publicly again. The minority that was 25% of the population is now 2% of the population. Although the census officially says 0%. The governor-general needs to be able to say that he successfully eliminated the Cedrians. And the people all thought their Cedrian neighbors to be all but eliminated.

37 years in hiding. And then it happened. A soldier was exploring the Northern Ridge of the Andonese Mountains when he found them. And the Cedrians prepared to evacuate their secret mountain hideout.

Bam! Bam! Machine gun fire was exchanged. Provincial troop reinforcements would be arriving shortly. The Cedrians defended their positions, but alas – their rifles were 37 years old.

The first helicopter was boarding, ready to take as many Cedrians as could be crammed in to their far-away safety destination. Aristide, a ranking member of the Cedrian civil defense committee, hooked up his radio, as he had been training for 37 years, awaiting this fateful moment of getting as many people to safety as possible. "Ludwig, do you hear me?" "Aristide, copy 5x5. At the Northern Ridge, things are getting critical." Machine gun fire was making it hard for Aristide to hear Ludwig on the radio. Ludwig continued to speak. His voice was raised not so it could be heard over the gunfire, but simply out of panic. "The provincial guard's reinforcements have arrived. We are losing men left and right. We're holding out as best we can but won't last much longer. As soon as the planes get here we are told they will be bringing heavy bombers. Send out the helicopters to evacuate civilians as outlined in our escape protocol. Today's the day, man. Let's make our future Cedrian generations proud. Today is our time to shine. Over and out." "Over and out," Aristide replied, then turned back to the evacuation helicopter.

Three members of the Cedrian civil defense committee were pushing – shoving – their people into the helicopter. The goal is to fit as many civilians onto the helicopter without having so many that the helicopter is weighted down and can't fly.

"Ok, that's it. We're full. Let 'er rip."

"No!! No!!" a woman cried. "Daniel!! Daniel!! If he's not going to live, I'm not going!" She tried to jump off the helicopter to be with her lover. It would be better to die together than to live the rest of her life without him.

Aristide said, "There will be another trip. We just need this full one to leave now so we can drop you all off at the secret safety destination and come back.

"Daniel!"

"Christine, stay on the helicopter!!"

"No, Daniel! Not without you!"

Daniel suddenly saw his brother, sitting next to Christine on the helicopter. The brothers' eyes met. Without uttering a word, they both communicated, and Daniel's brother knew what to do. Daniel nodded, to thank him to infinity.

Christine jumped, to be reunited with her lover. Daniel's brother immediately reached out and grabbed her by the arms, pulling her back on board.

"Daniel! Daniel!" she screamed.

The two lovers would never be reunited. Daniel died that day. As soon as the provincial air force arrived, those who had not left on the first 3 trips of the escape helicopter never left alive.

But who died? Was it Daniel? Or Christine? Daniel is in peace, in everlasting life, no more suffering or pain. He leaves this world knowing he has saved his lover's life.

Christine lives yet she is dead. Her lover who she has devoted her life to has perished. What good is it to live if you cannot love?

Her memory of Daniel – who gave his life for hers – shines bright in her heart. And she knows that soon she will join him for eternity.

But enough about 2 individuals. This is the whole Cedrian nation that is at stake. Let us return to their situation.

"Aristide! The provincial air force! They're here!"

"Copy 5x5. Ludwig, how many are there?"

"They're coming *en masse*. Aristide!! Shut the gate! Seal the escape module and push the self-destruction button for our classified library. Execute protocol 571. Look out for –"

Suddenly, boom. Another explosion. Boom, boom. Then: static.

Ludwig was no more. Nor was the radio control base at the Northern Ridge. The Cedrians had a short time to board the third – and last – escape helicopter.

Panic ensued. "Order! Order!" Aristide screamed. Fellow Cedrians fought for a spot on this last helicopter – and fought for their life.

"Ok, that's it. Any more and she won't be able to fly."

The pilot nodded. "All aboard!" And the helicopter took off. Cedrians grabbed ahold of the landing gear, desperately trying to get out before the provincial guard arrives – or the provincial air force bombs them out – or both.

A mother who was not on the helicopter lifts her baby – only 1 year old – and places it in the arms of a man and woman on the helicopter. Before they could say no – before they could return the baby to its owner – the helicopter took off. There was no turning back. The man and woman looked back at the mother. The gaze in her eyes said it all. Save her life. Raise her. Then: ka-boom. The provincial air force zoomed overhead and dropped enough bombs to destroy New York and Los Angeles at the same time. The helicopter survived but no one else did. Including the baby's mother. The 2 people holding the baby watched as she suddenly disappeared into the smoke and fire of the explosion. There was no family planning. They were parents now and loved their baby girl with all their heart. At the new secret safety location, the Cedrians sealed their gates. They stuck together as a community. The baby grew to a girl to a woman. She lived a long, happy life with her new loving family. 37 years passed. The Cedrians waited for the future, planning their next escape and vowing to keep hiding.

A Mysterious Evening in Vienna

The man in the three-piece suit proceeded through the elaborate corridors in the Hapsburg Palace in Vienna. Not proudly, but silently, lurking in the shadows of mystery and despair mixed with the wrath of doubt and uncertainty. Where was this man going? What was at the end of the long, ornate corridor that was slowly yet surely coming to an end? Why was he all dressed up?

"Monsieur Witherson! I am so happy to see you! I've been worried that you haven't come by in weeks!" spoke a voice from the left. Colonel Witherson turned and saw Mademoiselle Céline Fantouille. Witherson paused. He stood there, head turned towards Fantouille, not muttering a single audible word. His lips did not move, but inside, his heart was melting. His breath skipped a beat for a moment. "Céline, I told you not to-" Mademoiselle Fantouille approached Colonel Witherson slowly but bravely. She had her heart in her eyes and the weight of the universe in her head. "Richard, where have you been?"

"My dear, dear, dear Céline. My heart, my mind, my soul will miss you. I –" The question "Why have you not been coming to see me?" was suddenly answered. Céline knew. Colonel Witherson had been sent to another city. Another country. Another universe.

Immediately, she was presented with the next question of whether or not he will ever come back. Céline looked into Richard's eyes. She gazed into his deep brown eyes. She peered into his eyes, his brain, his mind, his soul. For a man of mysteries, there was, sadly, no mystery here. Colonel Witherson's gaze was sad, knowing that the two would be parted indefinitely. Would the future be kinder than the current predicament that exists to infinity? Could infinity be long enough to reunite the two?

The colonel took his hat off, lowered his head and gazed towards the floor. "Richard! Richard! Richard! I will miss you. I love you. I will love you forever. How I will miss you." "Céline, that is why I haven't seen you. It was too difficult for me to share the news with you of my reassignment. I don't think we will ever see each other again. I will miss you too much to ever be able to say goodbye to you, so I have avoided this terrible moment. Adieu will only cause more pain and unneeded suffering."

"Where will you go?" asked Céline.

"I will receive my new assignment on Thursday. It will be a secret mission this time, reporting directly to the ministry of foreign affairs division of army intelligence. I will not know my new country until Thursday. The suspense of not knowing where I will be is killing me. But please know that, come Thursday, the sorrow and pain within me will only get worse, because I will not be allowed to tell you. How I wish I could tell you. My dear Céline, if there were anyone on this earth that I would wish to tell, it would be – "

"Frauline Kleipst!"

The door to the end of the corridor opened. A clean-cut, formally-dressed German diplomat came through the door. "Good evening, Richard." "Hello." "Good evening, Céline." "Guten Abend." Frauline Kleipst turned back to Richard. But he was nowhere to be found. Frauline Kleipst turned around; to her left; to her right. "That's odd. He was just here. Where did Richard run off to?" She was dumbfounded. But Céline understood. Sometimes, rather than suffer through the pain of words, it is better to depart into the shadows of the abyss.

.

Arrival in Istanbul

The accountant stepped off the plane in Istanbul. Ready to embark on shady corporate off-shore tax bookkeeping for the multinational factory.

He looked at the "Welcome to Istanbul" sign.

"Damn! I thought I was going to Constantinople," he mused in lost confusion.

A Turk turned to him and said, "Istanbul *is* Constantinople. Same thing, different name."[6]

"Oh. That clarifies things. Thanks."

The accountant proceeded to baggage claim, where he waited patiently for his suitcase to arrive on the carousel. How much did he pack in his suitcase? Did he have 2 bags? 1 bag? Was it heavy?

Actually, it was empty. The accountant had brought one empty suitcase for his month-long stay on an international trip. After all, what do you need?

For work, he had his laptop. That's all you need to exchange data, use Excel, keep corporate records and save documents. So he

---

[6] See song: They Might Be Giants, "Istanbul (not Constantinople)," *Flood* (1990), Accessed June 15, 2017, https://genius.com/They-might-be-giants-istanbul-not-constantinople-lyrics.

brought his laptop in his carry-on. But why the empty suitcases? What about clothing and toothbrush and razor and shoes and dress shirts and tie?

"The Turkish lira is so cheap that it's more efficient to just buy clothing for my trip when I get here. The credit cards that I have in my wallet take up a lot less room and the dollar is stronger than the lira. The empty suitcase is for souvenirs to bring back home."

The accountant, with only the one suit, tie and shirt on his back, proceeded to the hotel. He looked at the counter of the hotel's front desk. There was coffee and Turkish delights on the welcome table. Although, in Turkish, they don't call them "Turkish delights." Just "delights." Money can't buy you happiness, but it can buy you a lot of delight.

"Hello," said the desk clerk. "Welcome to Istanbul formerly known as Constantinople. How can I help you?"

"Checking in, for Larry Coubarbu." And he took his very, very, very light suitcase up to the third floor room and prepared for tomorrow.

Postface

I chose September 3rd for the date of publication of *A Mysterious Evening in Vienna*. This is my first published book, and in a sense is the debut of my voice as a writer. My fellow history nerds know that September 3, 1939 was when France and England declared war on Nazi Germany. Prime ministers Édouard Daladier and Neville Chamberlain, who both shook hands with Hitler at the Munich Conference just 1 year earlier, are now drawing the line and declaring war on Hitler - in a sense creating their voice and speaking up for what is right. This is also the date of the king's speech from the movie *The King's Speech*. A king who cannot talk suddenly has a voice. George VI's speech impediment is no longer an impediment for him to have a voice. When war is declared, the British king is able to articulate his speech on live radio that resonates his voice worldwide. Democracy speaks out against fascism, and a previously-unheard voice is debuted. What better day to publish and let my writing speak its voice for the first time? But yet is that not the purpose of writing? To insert your voice into the world of words. To let your voice be heard. To speak up. So make your contribution to the world of literature. Stop thinking and start sharing. Insert your voice into the dialogue. The world will never be the same.

JOHN R. TEEVAN III

48

Bibliography

Derrida, Jacques & Élisabeth Roudinesco. *For What Tomorrow ... A Dialogue*. Jeff Fort (Translator). (Stanford, CA: Stanford University Press, 2004).

Harper, Douglas. *Online Etymology Dictionary.* s.v. "republic." Accessed August 8, 2017. http://www.etymonline.com/index.php?term=republic&allo wed_in_frame=0.

The King's Speech. DVD. Directed by Tom Hooper. (London, UK: UK Film Council, 2010).

They Might Be Giants. "Istanbul (not Constantinople)." *Flood* (1990). Accessed June 15, 2017. https://genius.com/They-might-be-giants-istanbul-not-constantinople-lyrics.

About the Author

John R. Teevan III is a writer, traveler, dreamer and artist. He completed a Bachelor's Degree in French, graduating *summa cum laude* from the University at Albany, State University of New York. He studied abroad in Paris at France's prestigious Sorbonne University. John went on to complete a Master's Degree in French and another Master's Degree in Teaching English to Speakers of Other Languages, both from the University at Albany, SUNY. In addition to writing, John loves to travel the world, draw, meet new people, learn foreign languages and immerse himself in a new and exciting foreign culture.

www.JTeevanWriter.weebly.com

John would love to hear from you. You can reach out to him at: JTeevanWriter@gmail.com

Made in the USA
Middletown, DE
05 September 2017